Flora is going to visit the zoo.

Who will she see first?

There are lots of animals to see.

Where is Puppy?

First a stripy tiger with her playful cubs.

Whose trunk is that?

Next a very tall giraffe eating some leaves.

Can you see the bird?

And an elephant with a bendy trunk.

Who has sharp claws?

Then a pretty parrot sitting on her perch.

Whose leg is this?

And a friendly brown bear with sharp claws.

Who is playing in the waves?

A slithering snake winding up a tree.

Who is about to hatch?

And two sea lions splashing in the waves.

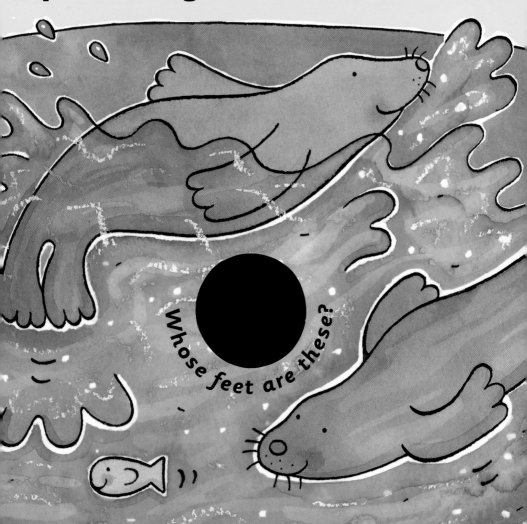

Whose feet are these?

And a family of penguins going for a walk.

Who is waiting for Flora?

What a lovely day!
It's time to go home
to Puppy.

Goodbye animals!